TaleSpinners I

S0-BZB-834

*Balloon Spies*

Dudley Bromley

A Pacemaker® Book

FEARON EDUCATION
a division of

PITMAN LEARNING, INC.

Belmont, California

## TaleSpinners™ I

### Balloon Spies

Better Than New

Death Angel

Dream Pirate

Golden God

Johnny Tall Dog

The Joker

Man in the Cage

Senior development editor: Christopher Ransom Miller

Content editor: Carol B. Whiteley

Production manager: Patricia Clappison

Design manager: Eleanor Mennick

Cover and text designer: Innographics

Cover and text illustrator: Christa Kieffer

ISBN–0–8224–6730–5
Library of Congress Catalog Card Number:
80–65914
Printed in the United States of America.

1.9 8 7 6 5 4 3 2 1

# Contents

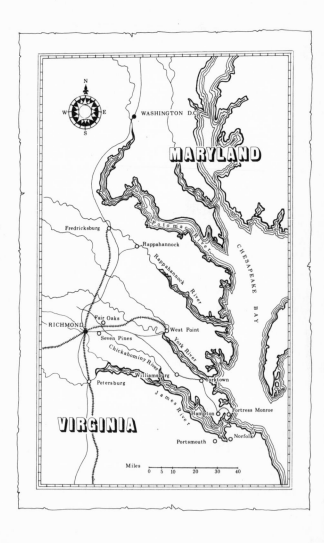

# 1

# Air Show

*Many young men would soon be leaving the city. The Civil War had started only three months before, on April 19, 1861. It was calling them away.*

*The people of Columbus, Ohio, wanted to give their young men a send-off that would be talked about for years. They held a daylong Fourth of July picnic at the fairgrounds. There was a square dance too, and a fireworks show. It was a beautiful day. Everyone in town came to join in the excitement.*

Floating in the center of the fairgrounds, the balloon called the *Benjamin Franklin* could be seen for miles. Taller than the tallest tree, it looked like a giant red, white, and blue bag. Lighter-than-air coal gas kept the balloon inflated and floating. And two strong lines tied it to the ground. Most of the day, the *Benjamin Franklin* had been hanging there in all its bright beauty. It was a sure sign that something special was happening in Columbus.

The giant balloon had drawn a large crowd. People were feeling very excited. An army band was playing, and everywhere there were young men in blue uniforms. They would soon be going away to fight in the war against the South. But now they gathered with the other people of Columbus to look at the amazing balloon.

At the back of the crowd stood the balloon's owners. Oren and Lillian Barth watched the excitement grow. They waited for the signal that would tell them to begin the air show. Though it was a warm day, both Lillian and Oren wore big hats and long coats. They didn't want anyone to see their costumes. That would let the crowd know that they were part of the show.

As they waited, Oren turned suddenly to his wife. He looked very worried. "Did we pack Elmo?" he asked.

Lillian shook her head and smiled. "You ask that before every ascension, Oren. Yes, Elmo's all packed and ready to go. Everything is fine. It's going to be a great show."

Suddenly half a dozen horns sounded. It was the signal for the show to begin. Dropping their hats and coats to the ground, Oren and Lillian ran to the front of the crowd. They smiled and waved. The friendly people of Columbus cheered them more loudly than any other crowd they had ever played to.

Without his hat and coat, Oren really stood out. He was not a tall man, but he was very strong. And he looked it. He was also completely bald, though he had a long moustache he kept carefully waxed. With his cape and bright red and gold costume, Oren looked as if he had just dropped in from another world.

Lillian stood out too. She was tall and fair, with long blonde hair and sky-blue eyes. Like Oren, she wore a cape over a bright red and gold costume. And like Oren, she was a crack balloonist.

The crowd wanted the show to begin. With a final wave to the people, Oren stepped into the balloon's "car," or gondola. This was the four-foot-square wicker basket where the balloonists rode. The basket was perfect for ballooning. The wicker was light yet strong. It was strong enough to carry three people and several 100-pound bags of sand. When the bags were dropped over the side, the balloon would rise higher. The gondola was tied to the heavy rope netting that covered the balloon.

"Hello, Elmo." Oren spoke in a low voice as he climbed into the gondola. If anyone had heard him, they would have wondered whom he was talking to because no one else could be seen in the gondola, but Oren said hello anyway. Then he turned to see Lillian climbing in next to him.

Once Lillian was inside, Oren cut one of the lines that held the *Benjamin Franklin* to the ground. This was a signal that all was ready. A man on the ground quickly untied the end of the second line. The crowd grew quiet as the great balloon slowly rose into the air. Then the people burst into a loud cheer. Horses reared, and chickens ran in fear across the field.

Up the balloon climbed, higher and higher, until it rested hundreds of feet above the excited crowd. Finally it seemed to stop climbing. Everyone below watched to see what would happen next. Suddenly a frightening yell came down from above. Then someone in the crowd called out, "Oh, no! One of them is falling! Look out!"

People started screaming as a figure in a red and gold costume came falling toward them. Children began to cry. A few quick-thinking people rushed around getting everyone out of the way of the falling balloonist.

Just above the tops of the trees, however, the falling figure was jerked to a sudden stop. More screams rang out. Many people turned away or covered their eyes. They didn't want to see the terrible sight above them. But as soon as they stopped looking, they heard other people laughing.

Neither Oren nor Lillian was hanging from the long rope coming from the gondola. Instead a dummy hung there, dressed like the balloonists. And it had broken open when the rope had snapped it to a stop. Now hundreds of sheets of paper were spilling from its body. The papers rained down on the people below, who rushed about to see what was written on them.

Up in the gondola, Oren and Lillian leaned over the side to watch. Oren smiled. "Good old Elmo," he said. "He steals the show every time."

"And I'm glad he does," Lillian told him. Both she and Oren knew that without Elmo, their act probably couldn't go on. The papers the dummy had just delivered in such an exciting way were newspapers Oren and Lillian had printed. Elmo dropped *The Flying Times* halfway through each air show. The advertisements the paper carried paid for all the equipment to keep the show going.

Oren and Lillian watched the crowd a few moments longer. Then, with a sharp move of his arm, Oren reached up and pulled a red rope. The rope tore a hole in the bottom of the balloon. With a rush, the coal gas inside the *Benjamin Franklin* escaped. The giant balloon started to cave in and fall.

Once again the people on the ground screamed and ran for cover. But up in the gondola, Oren and Lillian did not act worried. They had done the same act at least 100 times before. They knew that the force of the air would push the bottom of the balloon up into the top. The *Benjamin Franklin* turned into a giant parachute and floated slowly back to earth.

As before, the crowd's fear turned to delight when they saw that no one would be hurt. They ran back smiling toward the balloon to cheer its passengers. The band struck up a happy marching song.

As the wicker gondola touched the ground, a tall young man was already waiting there. He was about Oren's age, and he introduced himself as Thaddeus Lowe. With a smile, he invited Lillian and Oren to join him for lunch. He said he wanted to talk to Oren.

Oren's mouth fell open. He couldn't find his voice, so he just nodded. Thaddeus Lowe was a very famous man. In the eyes of Oren and Lillian and most people, he was the best and most famous balloonist in America.

# 2

# Professor Lowe

*Thaddeus Sobieski Constantine Lowe was not like other balloonists of his day. He was trained as a scientist. He called himself an "aeronaut" and his balloon an "aerostat." He was also a teacher, an inventor, and a builder. During his life, he invented a machine for making ice and built the world's first refrigerator ship for carrying fresh foods across the ocean. He also built a famous railroad up the side of a mountain in Pasadena, California. But his great love was ballooning.*

*Before the Civil War, Professor Lowe had had a dream. He had dreamed of starting the world's first airline—made up of balloons. When the war broke out, Lowe put his dream away for a while. But as soon as the fighting was over, he planned to build dozens of giant balloons. Each one would have a gondola large enough to carry 100 people to any city in North America.*

Like everyone else at the picnic, Oren, Lillian, and Professor Lowe filled their plates with all kinds of good foods. They listened to some speeches telling the city's young men to fight bravely and bring the war to a quick end. Finally the three fliers made their way to a table. And there Oren and Thaddeus Lowe began trading balloon stories. As they ate, they described some of the wild balloon rides they had taken over the past few years.

Lillian couldn't decide which of the men was telling bigger lies. She knew for a fact that most of what Oren was telling Lowe just wasn't true. And Lillian was pretty sure that most of the professor's stories were tall tales too. She shook her head and tried to keep a straight face.

Finally Lillian had had enough. The meal was long over. It looked like the storytelling might go on for hours. As soon as Oren finished his latest hair-raising tale, she broke in. She asked Lowe why he had wanted to meet with Oren.

"Yes, it's time we got around to business," Lowe said to her. Then he leaned across the table toward Oren and spoke in a low voice. "Three weeks ago, I met with President Abraham Lincoln at the White House."

Lillian and Oren stared at the professor with surprise. But he kept on talking in a quiet way.

"I showed the president a new kind of aerostat I've built. It's a war balloon," he went on. "I also suggested that a Balloon Corps made up of these aerostats could be useful in the war against the South. The president agreed. And he put me in charge of finding the aeronauts for the corps."

Lillian's heart started pounding. Suddenly she knew the reason for Professor Lowe's visit. He was going to ask Oren to become one of the aeronauts.

"It sounds very interesting," Oren said as Lillian looked over at him. "Please, Professor —tell me more."

Professor Lowe moved even closer to Oren. "Aeronauts will be paid by the government," he said. "But they will remain civilians. In their balloons they'll have two jobs: watching the enemy and making maps. And there will be a telegraph on board each war balloon for sending the findings to the army below."

Lillian couldn't stand it any longer. Lowe's words were exciting—but he was speaking only to Oren! She cleared her throat and held up her hand. "I want to say something," she broke in.

"Just a minute, Lil," Oren said without so much as a look in her direction. Lillian's eyes blazed, but Oren's were locked on Professor Lowe. "Wouldn't cameras be important too? Aeronauts could take pictures of the enemy as well. That way the generals could see where the enemy was for themselves."

Thaddeus shook his head. "It makes more sense for a general who wants to see the enemy to go up in a balloon himself. It takes too long for pictures to be printed. No, photography is not yet ready to be useful as a tool of war. In another few years, perhaps."

As soon as Lowe finished talking, Lillian started to speak up again. But once more Oren jumped in ahead of her. "Well, have you thought of this?" he asked the professor. "A free-flying balloon could fire on the enemy!"

"Yes, I thought of it," Lowe answered quickly. "But as soon as I did, I forgot it. It's too dangerous. All Balloon Corps aerostats will be tied down—they will go on no free flights. There's no way to know where a free-flying balloon will come down. And it goes without saying what would happen to a Union aeronaut forced down behind Rebel lines. Only a fool would try to fly near the enemy, even to fire at them. And I don't plan to pick any fools to fly my balloons."

"I take it then, Professor, that you're asking me to join your Balloon Corps." Oren spoke quickly, before Lillian could get in a word.

Lillian hit the table with her hand. She knew it was too late for her to say anything now. Lowe answered Oren's question right away.

"Indeed," he said. "You know, there aren't more than half a dozen good aeronauts in the whole country. And I feel, Oren, that you're one of them. With aeronauts like you, the Balloon Corps can help the Union win the war. If you join me, you'll be part of history. What do you say?"

Oren smiled. "I say I'd like to give it a try," he answered. "But I'm part of a team. Lillian and I work together. She knows every bit as much about ballooning as I do. Since you want only the best aeronauts, I know you'll want Lillian to join the corps as well."

Now it was Lillian's turn to smile. She looked at Professor Lowe. He pulled on his moustache and thought for a moment. "Why not? Some of the generals may not like the idea of a woman balloonist. But you'll still be civilians, even though you'll be working for the army. So it won't matter if the generals don't like it." He turned to Lillian. "I hope you'll join the corps as well."

Oren and Lillian looked at each other and smiled again. Then they looked at Professor Lowe.

"When do we leave?" they said together.

# 3

# **Balloon Corps**

*The Civil War has been called the first modern war, and with good reason. For the first time, railroads played an important part in a war. So did steam-powered ships, and ironclads—ships covered with iron armor. So did the telegraph. And science had also made possible all kinds of new weapons. From breechloading artillery and small arms to Richard Gatling's famous machine gun, these new weapons resulted in the deaths of over 600,000 people.*

*The Civil War was also the very first war that moved from land and sea into the air. Airplanes were not yet flying. But both sides had an air force—of balloons.*

Oren and Lillian didn't hear from Thaddeus Lowe again for almost a year. But they had known it would take him time to get the Balloon Corps ready, Then early in the spring of 1862, a young Union soldier came up to them as they finished an air show in Baltimore. The soldier gave them a note from Professor Lowe.

"To Aeronauts Barth," the note said. "At last the Balloon Corps is ready to fly. Report at once to Admiral Preston C. Forsyth, U.S. Navy, Washington, D.C."

Oren looked up from the note and shook his bald head. He eyed the soldier. "Navy?" he asked.

The soldier nodded. "Yes, sir. General McClellan has loaded his whole army—112,000 men—onto boats! Horses, cannons, everything! He's shipped them all down the Potomac, then down Chesapeake Bay to Fortress Monroe. They're on Rebel soil now, and McClellan is marching them straight for Richmond. The war will probably be over before summer is through."

"Then we had better hurry," said Lillian. And hurry they did. After putting their few things together, Lillian and Oren first reported to Admiral Forsyth. Then they were sent over the same route that McClellan's army had followed. They were put on a ship and taken south to Fortress Monroe, deep in the heart of the Confederacy.

Though in Rebel territory, Fortress Monroe always stayed under Union control. It was in a very important place, on the end of a peninsula near the mouth of Chesapeake Bay. The York River that flowed to the north of the peninsula was also controlled by the Union. But the James River to the south was under Rebel control. It was from Fortress Monroe that McClellan had started his strong Army of the Potomac marching toward Richmond.

Fortress Monroe served as a main supply station for the army. But with its high stone walls and wide moat, it looked more like a castle than an army base. Oren and Lillian were met at its gates by a small company of Union guards. Right away the guards put them and their belongings in a wagon. In the wagon they traveled three miles north to Hampton.

It was after dark when they arrived. By the light of several fires, they could see hundreds of soldiers camped outside the city. These were the rear guard of McClellan's army. The main body of the army was more than 10 miles north on its way to attack Yorktown.

The wagon stopped finally in front of a small tent. The guards helped Oren and Lillian down with their things. After watching the wagon drive off in a cloud of dust, the tired aeronauts looked around their new home. It wasn't much, but it was a place to sleep. A small meal was all they had energy for before climbing into bed.

But they didn't sleep for long. Before the sun was even up, two figures walked quickly up to the tent. One of the early visitors was Brigadier General Alva Merriweather Cooper. The other was Cooper's aide, Lieutenant Malcomb Thomas Anderson, who carried a small lantern.

Cooper was an army man through and through. He had joined up during the War of 1812, nearly 50 years before. He didn't care much for the new war equipment the leaders in Washington kept sending him. As a matter of fact, General Cooper wasn't sure about anything anyone called "modern."

"Mr. Barth!" the general shouted into the opening of Lillian and Oren's tent. "Come out of that tent in one minute, if you will!"

Oren stepped into the cold early morning darkness well before his time was up. He was buttoning his shirt and blinking his eyes. "What is it?" he asked. "What's wrong?"

"Are you Barth, sir?" the general asked.

Oren locked his eyes on the man who stood before him. He saw gold stars on the man's hat and coat. He was sure the steady look he was receiving was from someone important. But he didn't care. He was angry at the way he had been called out of bed.

"Yes, I'm Barth." Oren answered in a voice that was as loud as the general's. "Who the devil are you?"

Lieutenant Anderson answered Oren's question. "You are speaking to Brigadier General Alva M. Cooper!" he called out.

General Cooper started talking again right away. He walked slowly back and forth in front of Oren. "I was having breakfast a few minutes ago," he said. "Lieutenant Anderson here told me that the aeronauts had arrived. So I came right over to see what you look like. The people in Washington tell me that you can *fly,* Barth. They tell me that you're going to help us get information about the enemy. Well, it all sounds fine. But I don't believe anything unless I see it with my own eyes."

"I don't blame you, General," Oren said with a smile. He had stopped feeling angry at the general's strange way of meeting people. He was ready to do what he loved most—go up in a balloon. "I'll be happy to show you that people can indeed fly above the clouds. I trust that Professor Lowe has already sent the equipment?"

"It's here, all right. Been taking up space for more than a week," the general told him.

"Good. So as soon as I can get set up—"

"How long will that take?" General Cooper broke in.

Oren raised his arms and shook his head. "That will depend on the crew."

"Crew? What crew?" General Cooper stopped walking and stared right into Oren's face.

Oren looked back at him. "There's supposed to be a ground crew to help me inflate and raise the balloon."

"Nobody told me. I don't know anything about a crew," the older man said.

"Then I'll have to train one," Oren told him. "I'll need six men."

"You can have four."

"But, General—" Oren began.

"Four is all I can spare. Now how soon can you fly?"

Oren shook his head again. "I don't know. A few hours, maybe."

General Cooper took out his watch and looked at the time. He nodded. "I want a written report of your first flight on my desk by 10 o'clock."

"By 10?" Oren stepped closer to the older man and pointed to the tent. "If you don't mind, we're a bit tired from—"

"We?" General Cooper said. "Why, of course!" he went on suddenly. "Your wife is with you. Didn't I hear that she's an—"

The general's sentence was finished for him. "She's an aeronaut too," Lillian said as she stepped out of the tent. "You'll have your report by 10, General."

General Cooper shook his head. "A woman aeronaut," he said. "Why, the idea. . . ." He shook his head again, then looked at Lillian and Oren. "Well, man or woman, it remains to be seen whether any aeronauts will have a place in my army." He nodded quickly to Lillian. Then he turned, coughed loudly, and marched away into the darkness.

# 4

# Eyes in the Sky

The Union's war balloons were all built at Professor Lowe's aerostat factory in Philadelphia. Each had four 5,000-foot lines, five miles of insulated telegraph cable, a dozen flares, and a strong oxygen-hydrogen light to use during night flights. The floor of every gondola was fitted with a heavy armor plate to stop bullets fired from below.

The balloons were inflated with a machine called a "field generator." It had been invented by Professor Lowe to make inflating much faster. Inside each generator were small pieces of iron covered with water. When sulfuric acid was added, hydrogen—the lightest gas known—was released. This gas was used to fill the giant balloons.

*Thanks to Professor Lowe's field generator, balloons could be filled almost anywhere in a couple of hours. But this new way of filling balloons was also very dangerous. No fires of any kind could be allowed near the generators or the balloons. Even a tiny spark could cause the hydrogen to explode.*

"The general will see you now," Lieutenant Anderson said to Lillian and Oren. The two aeronauts nodded to the aide. Then they stepped inside General Cooper's tent.

The general sat behind a long table, looking through a pile of papers and maps. As he worked, he puffed on a pipe. "Yes," he said without looking up.

"We came to make our report, General," Oren said.

"Now?" The general looked up at his visitors. He nodded, then waved his hand. "Yes, well. Let's have it," he said quickly.

Oren handed the general several papers. "You'll see in our report that the telegraph for our balloon didn't work. The battery was dead."

"I'm not surprised," General Cooper barked. He took the papers and tossed them on the table without looking at them. Then he pointed a finger at Oren. "Machines are made to break down, young man," he said. "The sooner you understand that fact, the better off you'll be in this life."

"You may be right, General." Oren answered quickly, trying to keep the older man from going off into his usual storm of words. Oren went on, giving the general more papers as he talked.

"I thought you might like to take a look at these drawings also. Lillian made them. They show what we saw from our balloon in every direction."

The general looked at Lillian as he held the papers in his hand. "You're an artist as well as a aeronaut?"

Lillian smiled. "Why, yes, General," she said.

General Cooper shook his head as he looked at the first drawing in his hand. Then he asked in surprise, "You could see all the way across the bay?"

"We could see twice that far," Lillian told him.

General Cooper went on to the next drawing. It was the view to the south, toward the

James River. "Is that Norfolk?" he asked Oren, pointing to the city in the drawing.

"Yes. And that's Portsmouth to the south."

The general asked no further questions for several minutes. He stayed bent over the second drawing, studying it carefully. Finally he pointed to it and asked Lillian a question. "What are these—right here?"

Lillian looked at the drawing. "I'm not really sure, General," she said. "They looked like boats. But they're so far away that—"

"Boats?" General Cooper asked, sitting up straight. "Boats? Sitting empty on the riverbank?"

"As I said, General, I'm not really—"

"Lieutenant Anderson!" the general yelled, jumping up from his chair. "I want a company of men ready to march in five minutes!" The surprised aide stepped into the general's tent only long enough to hear the order.

Lillian's drawings turned out to have reported an important piece of information. The objects she had seen were indeed boats. Rebel boats had come across the James River from Norfolk to find out how many Union soldiers were at Fortress Monroe. But General Cooper's men surprised the soldiers in a swamp before they got a chance to look. After a short battle, the Rebels headed back to their boats. They were never seen on the peninsula again.

With Lillian's discovery of the Rebel boats, General Cooper was a changed man. No longer did he think that war balloons were useless "modern" equipment. And no longer did he want to keep the aeronauts out of his army. Lillian and Oren became an important part of his team. The general told everyone about his "eyes in the sky."

General Cooper even became interested enough in balloons to go up in one himself. He wanted to see what things looked like from the air. Early one morning, the general, Lieutenant Anderson, and Oren stepped into the gondola of the giant black and gray government balloon called the *Republic*.

"Stand by your cables!" Oren yelled to his crew. The aerostat pulled at its cables and moved in the light wind. Then the crew started letting the cables out to their full length. Slowly the *Republic* lifted its three passengers into the sky. At 1,500 feet, Oren signaled the crew to tie the cables fast. Soon after that, the black and gray balloon was floating like a cloud high above the peninsula.

"Well, what do you think of it?" Oren asked.

"It's so quiet," said Lieutenant Anderson as he looked all around.

"Pretty cold up here," the general barked. With a smile he added, "But what a sight."

"If you'll look through your field glasses, I'll point out a few places of interest," Oren said. He raised his own glasses. "Now over there, of course, is Fortress Monroe. Beyond it is the mouth of the James and—well, what is that?"

"General," said Lieutenant Anderson. He and the general were both looking through their glasses. They both saw what Oren had been talking about. "Isn't that—"

"By George, it is!" General Cooper said. He pounded the edge of the gondola with his fist.

"What is it?" Oren asked. "Is it that ship you're talking about?"

"Yes," answered Lieutenant Anderson in an excited voice. "But that's not just any ship. That's the *Merrimack*."

Oren took a deep breath. The *Merrimack* had been one of the best steamships in the American navy before the war. But it had been stationed at the Norfolk navy yard, which had ended up inside the Confederacy. To keep the ship out of Rebel hands, the Union forces had sunk it. But that wasn't the end of its life. The Confederates had raised the ship. Then they had covered its sides with heavy iron armor and named it the *Virginia*. But to the Union, the famous ironclad would always be the *Merrimack*.

The month before, in March 1862, the *Merrimack* had sailed into battle alone against the Union navy. It had sunk two of the wooden ships by ramming them. And it had sent all the others steaming for safety. Later that same month, the *Merrimack* had fought another sea battle that became one of the most famous in American history. In that battle, the ironclad *Merrimack* had met the Union's own ironclad, the *Monitor*.

*The Monitor* was a small ship—less than a third the size of the *Merrimack*. But the Union ironclad could do something no other ship in the world could do. It could fire its two big cannons in any direction.

The battle between the ironclads had lasted for more than four hours. Again and again the ships had fired at each other. Much of the time they were at close range. Finally they had both pulled back, with only a few dents to show for the battle. The meeting had ended in a draw. But it had changed the way sea battles would be fought in the years to come. Never again would a war be fought with ships made only of wood.

Ever since that famous battle, the *Merrimack* had guarded the mouth of the James River. It kept the river safely in the hands of the Confederacy. The *Monitor,* meanwhile, was always on the move, going from one end of Chesapeake Bay to the other. In this way, the small ironclad was able to keep that important water route open for Union ships. The two ships kept their distance. But everyone agreed it was just a matter of time before they would meet again.

As Oren and his passengers watched, it seemed the meeting was about to take place. From the balloon, they could see the *Merrimack* moving slowly toward Fortress Monroe. And they could see what the big ship was after. The *Monitor* was making a wide circle in the bay just off the end of the peninsula!

"Well, well, well," said General Cooper, banging his fist on the gondola again. "I do believe we are about to see the second battle between the ironclads!"

But the meeting was something less than a battle, and it was over in minutes. The *Merrimack* fired on the Union ship several times. But the *Monitor* did not return the fire. The Union ironclad just continued its circle, as if nothing was happening. So when the *Monitor* started back up the bay, the *Merrimack* just returned to its place guarding the James.

"Too bad, too bad," General Cooper said. "I would like to have seen the *Monitor* take the Rebs on." The general could not know then, but another battle between the ironclads would never take place. The *Monitor* was soon to sink during a storm. And the *Merrimack* would be sunk again, this time by the Confederates pulling out of Norfolk.

As General Cooper and his aide watched the two ships move farther apart, Oren was watching something else—lightning. He saw a flash of it to the west. That was enough to send him calling orders to his ground crew to lower the balloon quickly.

By the time the gondola touched down, a strong wind was blowing. Soon rain began to fall. Lieutenant Anderson and the general headed for their tents. But Oren stayed behind to watch his crew let the gas out of the *Republic* and pack the big balloon away. The rain grew stronger and the sky darker as the men worked.

Suddenly Oren heard Lillian shouting to him. He turned and saw her running toward him, pointing to his right. Not understanding her words through the storm, Oren looked to his right. What he saw was a young soldier carrying an oil lamp toward the balloon. The soldier probably wanted to give the workers some light in the growing darkness. But if he came too close, the oil lamp would cause the gas coming from the balloon to explode.

Oren started running toward the soldier, shouting at him to turn back. But it was too late. Before anyone else knew what was happening, the *Republic* blew up and turned into a giant ball of fire.

# 5

# Williamsburg

General McClellan knew that if he could capture Richmond, the Confederate capital, the
war would be over. But first he had to take
Yorktown, the strongest point in the Rebel
line. McClellan began to gather the biggest
cannons and more than 100,000 soldiers for
the attack on Yorktown. But it took weeks for
this strong army to be ready. And April
turned into May.

While McClellan put his army together,
Professor Lowe kept a balloon in the air over
the front line. He worked within a mile of the
Confederate cannons at Yorktown, getting information for McClellan—and being shot at
often.

Finally on May 4, the Union army was
ready. McClellan gave the order to attack, and

*the soldiers stormed the city. But when they
made their way into Yorktown, they found it
empty. The Confederates were gone. They
were retreating toward Richmond.*

*With shouts of joy, McClellan's army took
after the running Rebels. The Union soldiers
were sure the war was nearly over.*

Oren no longer had his long, waxed moustache, his pride and joy. The fire from the
exploding gas had burned it off. And if he had
not been bald already, he would have been
after the fire.

The explosion had been like a slap from a
giant's hand. Oren had been knocked out. His
moustache and clothes had been burned. But
somehow he had not been badly hurt. In fact,
no one had got more than small burns and
cuts. The balloon, however, was beyond re-
pair. It—or what was left of it—would never
fly again.

General Cooper stormed around all day
when he heard about the loss of the balloon.
He tried all day to get a new one sent to the
camp quickly. But he was told it would take
weeks or even months. Since time was so important, he asked the aeronauts to use their

own balloon, the *Benjamin Franklin*. He knew they had brought it with them.

At first Oren and Lillian didn't want to take a chance that something might happen to the balloon. It had cost them a lot of money. But General Cooper gave his word the army would pay for any damages. And soon after, they agreed to station the *Benjamin Franklin* above the camp.

It was several days, though, before they could do that. Bad weather kept the *Benjamin Franklin* grounded. When the sky finally cleared, Oren and Lillian began right away to get their aerostat ready to fly. But soon they were called to General Cooper's tent for a meeting.

The general was sitting behind his table, puffing on his pipe. "McClellan's taken Yorktown," he said in his quick way. He pointed for Oren and Lillian to sit down. "The Rebels are on the run. The whole Union army is giving chase. We've been ordered to move up the York River tomorrow toward West Point."

"While the main force marches on to Richmond, General?" Oren said.

"So it seems. We'll catch the Rebs between us. The war should be over before winter."

"It will be wonderful to look down at happy crowds again instead of people shooting each other," Lillian said.

"I have heard from Professor Lowe," General Cooper went on. "He sends word that he will be moving his balloon boat—whatever that is—up the York River near the front line. Before he leaves Yorktown tonight, he wants to see both of you. He has been able to get another government balloon. Looks like you won't have to use the *Benjamin Franklin* after all."

Oren and Lillian saw Professor Lowe's balloon boat when they reached Yorktown. It was a long, flat boat that had been used to carry coal before the war. Professor Lowe had cleaned it up and put in a new steam engine. He now used it to carry his heavy ballooning equipment across water. All that remained of the boat from before was its name, *G. W. Parke Custis,* painted on its side. The *G. W.* stood for George Washington.

Professor Lowe was too busy loading the boat to talk with his aeronauts for long. He did, however, say that General Cooper was turning in good reports on their work. He also gave them the new balloon to take the place of the *Republic*. After wishing their friend well, Oren and Lillian loaded the balloon, the *Phoenix*, onto their wagon and returned to camp. It was after midnight when they arrived, and they went right to bed. They knew the next day would begin early. And they were right.

The whole camp was up before the sun, getting ready to move out. Oren, Lillian, and their crew set about filling the *Phoenix* with hydrogen. Then they loaded their heavy equipment onto a wagon and tied the balloon to the back of it. As the soldiers moved out of the camp, Oren and Lillian climbed into the gondola. Then the balloon slowly lifted to the length of its lines. While the army marched, the two aeronauts would watch the road ahead.

They could see for miles. And what they saw was a line of marching Union soldiers that seemed to go on forever. Snaking across the ground, it looked as if it would never come to a stop. But before long it did. Then the thunder of cannons came rolling across the peninsula. Oren and Lillian saw smoke on the horizon. It looked like a battle was already beginning.

Spying Lieutenant Anderson below, Lillian quickly ordered the *Phoenix* brought down. She called out to the aide as the balloon was lowered. Then she ran with Oren toward the young man to find out what was happening.

"McClellan has caught the rear guard of the Confederacy at Williamsburg," he reported. "It's a bloody battle already, and it's just begun. Let us know what you see. I must go to General Cooper now."

Oren nodded as Lieutenant Anderson went quickly on his way. Then he turned to Lillian. "I'll go up alone this time," he said.

Lillian looked at him. His face seemed strange. "All right," she said slowly. Oren had gone up alone in the balloon before, And so had Lillian. But the two aeronauts usually worked together. This time, however, it seemed important to Oren to take the balloon up himself. "All right," Lillian said again. Oren nodded quickly. Then he climbed into the gondola.

# 6

# **Richmond**

The first leader of the Rebel forces at York-town had been Major General John Bankhead Magruder. His tiny Army of the Peninsula had numbered fewer than 12,000. Magruder, however, had soon been joined by General Joseph Johnston. Johnston's Army of Northern Virginia was made up of 50,000 seasoned soldiers. Magruder and Johnston knew a Union attack would come soon.

General Johnston had brought along something beside soldiers to help the forces at Yorktown get ready for the attack. He had brought along the South's own war balloon. It was made of cotton cloth and filled with hot air. The pilot of the unnamed balloon was a young captain, John Randolph Bryan. Bryan made several flights at Yorktown and was *often within sight of Professor Lowe's Balloon Corps. The Southern officer gave information to the leaders at Yorktown about the growing size of McClellan's army.*

*It was Bryan's information that made General Johnston see his army could not win against the Union forces at Yorktown. After a flight on May 2, 1862, Bryan reported that McClellan's army was almost twice as strong as Johnston's. The next day, Johnston decided to retreat. It has been said that this retreat saved the South from an early defeat in the war.*

Oren's plan was to find out where the Rebels were digging in and to report the news back to the Union. By doing this, he might save the lives of many soldiers. But he would have to make a free flight, no matter what Professor Lowe or anyone else had to say about it. So Oren waited until the *Phoenix* was in the air—then he cut the ropes. The *Phoenix* was flying free.

Two thousand feet below him, Oren could see the battle of Williamsburg being fought. The fight had not been under way long, but it

seemed to be almost over. The South was retreating, and the North was hot on its heels.
The big battle—when the South made its
stand—was yet to be fought.

For over an hour, the wind pushed the
*Phoenix* toward the west. Oren guessed that
he had moved about 50 miles in that time. He
also guessed that at that speed, he would
reach Richmond long before the front line of
the retreating Rebels.

But Oren didn't really think the South
would retreat all the way to Richmond. After
all, Richmond was their capital, the most important city in the South. The Rebel soldiers
would certainly try to keep the Union army
from getting close enough to attack it.

No, Oren was sure the Rebels would dig in
somewhere between Williamsburg and Richmond. He was so sure that he was putting his
own life in danger to prove it. Against Professor Lowe's orders—and against his own good
sense—he was flying the balloon over enemy
territory.

*Boom!*

At first, Oren thought the loud noise that
broke the quiet was thunder. He changed his

mind in a few seconds though. A big cannonball shot through the air close to his head.

The force of the wind in the cannonball's
wake almost pulled Oren out of the gondola.
Even worse, the *Phoenix* jerked to one side.
For a minute, Oren thought the balloon
would turn inside out and send him floating
into enemy hands. But finally the balloon
righted itself, and Oren looked over the side
and below.

He was deep into enemy territory. In fact
the soldiers below were so far from the Union
army they had felt safe enough to stop and
set up a cannon. It was the largest cannon
Oren had ever seen, and painted bright red.
And it was pointing straight up—right at the
*Phoenix.*

As Oren stared down into the open mouth
of the Rebel cannon, a cloud of white smoke
climbed into the air. For a moment he wondered what it was. He figured it out just before the noise from the cannon reached his
ears again.

*Boom!*

The smoke had come from the cannon fir-
ing right at Oren. As he straightened up in
surprise, a cannonball crashed into the

armor-plated bottom of the gondola. Oren was sure he was about to be killed. First there was a loud cracking sound. Then one end of the gondola shot up. Oren was tossed wildly around with everything else in the basket.

Before he knew what was happening, Oren grabbed a rope in front of him. As he held on, he was surprised to see the gondola falling away from him. In a moment, it jerked to a sudden stop at the end of its ropes. It was then that Oren discovered the cannonball had knocked him all the way up to the side of the balloon!

The cannonball had done something else as well. It had knocked some of the equipment out of the gondola. Now, with less weight to carry, the *Phoenix* was climbing higher and higher with the surprised Oren holding tightly to its side. Finally it stopped. Oren was able then to step down along the rope netting that covered the giant bag and jump into the gondola.

Finding his field glasses in the mess in the basket, Oren began studying the ground below. It seemed the *Phoenix* was more than a mile high now. It was still moving west. Oren

knew he would have to hurry. He wanted to
find the place where the Confederates would
stop and get back to the Union lines before
dark.

Far below, the line of Confederate soldiers
looked like a giant gray snake inching forward. The line wasn't stopping anywhere.
Nowhere did it look as if the Rebels were digging in. Could it be that Oren was wrong?
Would the Rebels really pull their whole
army back to Richmond?

As though in answer to his question, a
large city appeared on the western horizon. It
was Richmond. And the long gray line of soldiers was still moving slowly toward it.

But that wasn't all. Oren could also see a
large cloud of dust to the south of the city.
Another long gray line of soldiers was on the
move. They were coming to help defend the
Confederate capital.

The stand would be at Richmond, after all.
Oren had to get back to the Union army with
the news. The problem was that the *Phoenix*
was traveling west, and the Union forces lay
to the east. Oren would have to get the
*Phoenix* up higher and look for a wind to take

him east. He knew that winds blow in different directions at different altitudes. Throwing almost everything left in the gondola over the side, Oren sent the *Phoenix* climbing upward.

At 10,000 feet, Oren found his wind and headed east. Two hours later, he had reached the edge of Williamsburg. Pulling a rope to let some gas out of the balloon, he started to drop toward the ground. But to his surprise, he was met with gunfire.

The Union soldiers had seen the *Phoenix* coming from the west. It was no wonder they thought Oren was a Southern spy. And now they were trying to shoot him out of the sky!

# 7

# The Act

John Randolph Bryan was the first aeronaut in the Confederate air force. He made many flights for the Southern forces. But he lost his job suddenly one day. His balloon escaped its lines and with him in it crashed behind enemy lines. Bryan was able to get back to his own territory. But without his balloon, he never flew again.

Soon after that, however, the South built another aerostat. It was a beautiful balloon made of many different colors of fine silk. It is known that this silk balloon made several important flights at the bloody battle of Gaines Mill. But the names of the balloon and its pilot have been lost to history. In fact, very little is known about the Confederate air corps at all.

Lillian and General Cooper stood on a hill 10 miles west of Williamsburg. They were looking through their field glasses. They had seen Oren try to land the *Phoenix* and the Union soldiers open fire on him. Now they watched him cut the bottom out of the gondola, letting the heavy iron armor fall to earth. Suddenly much lighter, the *Phoenix* climbed quickly away from the heavy fire.

In a few moments, the *Phoenix* had moved much closer to Lillian and General Cooper. Now out of range of the soldiers, Oren tried to bring the big balloon down again. Pulling the rope that let the gas out, he headed for an open field to the south. But the wind was blowing hard. Oren couldn't control the landing. Lillian and General Cooper could only watch as the remains of Oren's gondola slammed into the ground.

But that wasn't the end. Suddenly the *Phoenix* was caught by the wind and shot up —across the James River and into enemy territory. Twisting and rolling, the big balloon flew over a deep woods and crashed far inside it. In moments it was gone from sight.

Lillian put down her glasses and turned toward the general. "I'm going after him,

General," she said. "I'm sure that he's alive."

"What did you say?" said General Cooper.

"I'm going after Oren," Lillian said again. "I wish I had a dollar for every time I've watched my husband make a bad landing and then found him safe and sound."

"But this is different," General Cooper yelled, hands on hips. "There's a war—"

"All the more reason for me to get started right away," said Lillian. She had her hands on her hips too.

General Cooper looked at the aeronaut in front of him. Then he thought for a moment. "All right," he agreed. "If you think you can find him. But I'm going to send a company of soldiers to guard you."

"No," Lillian said quickly. "I'm sure I'll have a better chance alone. All I need is a horse and wagon, a few pieces of furniture, and some blankets."

"Furniture? Blankets? What on earth are you planning to do?"

"Save my husband's life, I hope," Lillian told him.

Half an hour later, Lillian was ready to go in search of Oren. The general had found her a quiet horse and an old farm wagon. Because it was almost dark, she hung a lighted oil lamp on each side of the wagon. Then she gathered up the long skirt of her dress and climbed up to the seat. The dress felt strange after many months in her aeronaut's clothes. But the feel of the horse at the other end of the reins was just like old times. Years before, she had trained horses for her own circus act.

"Good boy," she said as the horse began to pull the wagon through the camp toward the James River. "We'll get Oren out no matter what happens."

At the river, a steam ferry waited for Lillian. Two soldiers met her and led the horse and wagon onto the boat. Then, with a puff of steam, the ferry began the trip across.

Lillian knew the roads were still open on the other side where the ferry would stop. But the area was filled with Rebel soldiers. So she had her plan all worked out before she landed. As soon as the ferry reached the far side, she drove off and down the road toward the woods. The ferry moved back out into the river. It would return the next night to pick her up.

For many hours, Lillian drove through the darkness with the tangle of trees on either

side. Only the small light from her oil lamps
showed her the roads as she made her way in
the direction of the *Phoenix*. Suddenly her
horse's head went up.

A man's deep voice called out, "Stop, or
we'll shoot!"

Lillian quickly stopped the wagon. In
seconds half a dozen Confederate soldiers
were all around her. Their horses were
crowding around the wagon. Standing up,
Lillian smiled at the soldiers in the lamp-
light. Then she looked their captain straight
in the eyes and smiled harder. "Am I ever
glad to see you, General," she said in her best
southern accent. She wondered if the soldiers
would believe she wasn't a Northerner.

"I'm just a captain, ma'am," the Confederate leader said. Lillian breathed again. Her
act was working—so far.

"I'm still glad to see you," Lillian went on.
"I was afraid you were Yankees at first. It
seems like the whole country is crawling
with Yankees."

"Yes, ma'am. And that brings me to won-
dering why you're out here all by yourself in
the middle of the night."

Sitting down on the wagon seat, Lillian
acted as if she was about to cry. "My husband

went off to fight the Yankees last month,"
she said. "I've been all alone ever since. The
war's been getting closer and closer. I finally
decided to pack up my most important belongings and get to Richmond before the
Yankees captured our farm. Who knows
what they would do if—"

"Yes, ma'am," the captain broke in. "I
think you made a wise decision. But why
didn't you start your trip sooner? If you had,
you could have reached Richmond before
dark."

Lillian shook her head and put her face in
her hands. "I started in the middle of the
day," she said. "But I got lost. And now I
think I'm lost again. I should have reached
Richmond already. I'm turned around, and I
don't know which way is which."

"Don't worry, ma'am," the Confederate
captain told Lillian. "I'll be glad to send two
of my best officers to ride along with you to
Richmond."

Lillian blinked and sat up straight. The
last thing she wanted was two Rebel soldiers
guarding her. "Oh, thank you, Captain," she
said. "But that really won't be necessary. I'm
sure your men have more important things to
do than help me. If you could just point me in

the right direction, I would be very grateful."

"Well, as a matter of fact, we are on our way to guard the road to Norfolk."

"Then don't let me keep you," Lillian said with her best smile. "Don't worry, Captain. I'll be fine."

"Yes, ma'am. Just go back down this road until another road goes off to the right. That other road is the one that leads to Richmond."

"Thank you, Captain. You've helped me so much. I'll be sure to go the right way."

"Yes, ma'am. Good night, ma'am."

"Good night, Captain," Lillian called. She waited until the horses could no longer be heard. Then she headed straight off the road and into a thick clump of brush and trees. She climbed down from the wagon and put out the oil lamps.

"That was pretty close," she said to the horse as she tied it to a tree. "Let's hide here until the first daylight comes. Then we'll go into the woods. Oren has to be close by." While the horse stood quietly in the darkness, Lillian changed into the farmer's clothes she had hidden in the wagon.

Soon the morning light touched the tops of the tall trees. Lillian unhitched the horse and swung up on its back. Slowly and carefully she crossed the road and entered the forest. She didn't know whether she would ever find the wagon again. But, she thought, let me find Oren first. Then I'll worry about the wagon.

As the horse picked its way through the dense brush, she looked up at the tops of the trees. She was trying to spot broken branches and bits of rigging. This was not the first time she had searched for Oren in the woods. She knew the signs to look for.

For over an hour, Lillian rode deep into the trees. No Oren. She was so tired she caught herself starting to slide off the horse. Then she heard the sound of other horses and riders close by. She jumped off and put her hand on the horse's nose to keep it quiet. The other riders never heard a sound. She stayed wide awake after that.

Finally, just when she was about to give up, Lillian spotted a large, dark shape hanging from a tree. Moving closer, she saw what it was—the torn remains of the *Phoenix*. On the ground, below the pieces of cloth, was Oren.

Lillian jumped down from the horse. She could see that Oren's eyes were closed and his bald head was black and blue. But she knew he was alive. Suddenly Oren's eyes opened. "Well, Lil," he said. "You've found me again." Then he smiled and shook his head. "And am I glad you did! With this broken leg, I couldn't even try to get back to the camp."

"I'm glad I found you too," Lillian said. She and Oren held each other for a moment. Then she said, "We'd better get going now. Rebel soldiers could find us at any minute."

She helped Oren pull himself up on the horse. Then she swung quickly up behind him. She knew that soon the pain and shock would catch up with Oren. And she did not know if she could find the wagon.

But the horse began to move without her showing it where to go. Carefully the big animal picked its way back through the trees. Lillian remembered that horses can usually find their way back, even when their riders are lost. This horse wasted no time. The road appeared sooner than Lillian had expected. She stopped to look around. Then she led the horse across and into the hiding place.

With Oren safely under blankets in the wagon, Lillian decided to rest until night came. The ferry would not return until after dark. And the Rebels were likely to be using the road by day.

Lillian had brought a little food and water. After Oren ate and got warm again, he began to feel better. The pain was no worse, and he drifted off to sleep.

That night Lillian hitched up the horse and changed into her dress. The time had come to return to the ferry at the James River.

CHAPTER

# 8

# Shenandoah

By the third week in May, McClellan's army was camped on both sides of the Chickahominy River near Richmond. But once again, the Union general waited to attack. This time he was waiting for General Irvin MacDowell's Army of the Rappahannock. It was marching south from Fredericksburg. With Mac-Dowell's help, McClellan was sure he could capture Richmond.

In the meantime, the Union was having troubles on another front. Not far to the west of Fredericksburg, Confederate General Thomas J. Jackson was attacking Union forces —and winning.

General Jackson had been called "Stonewall" Jackson ever since the First Battle of

*Bull Run. There he and his men had stood "like a stone wall" against the attacking Yankees. Now the general was making an even bigger name for himself in the Shenandoah Valley.*

*In fact, many Union leaders began to fear that Stonewall Jackson would soon march against Washington, D.C. President Lincoln was one of them. He decided late in May that something had to be done to stop Jackson—before it was too late.*

Three weeks had passed since Lillian had found Oren in the woods near the James River. The two aeronauts and their wagon had returned safely across the river. Then Oren had quickly told General Cooper that the Rebels were retreating all the way to Richmond.

Cooper was glad at Oren's return. But the news he brought turned out to be of little importance. When it had become clear that the Confederates would stand at Richmond, McClellan had given up the chase. He now sat waiting for more soldiers to arrive before marching against the city. No one knew how long that might take.

While everyone waited, Oren and Lillian spent most of their time playing cards in their tent. Oren still couldn't walk because of his broken leg. He played sitting up in bed while Lillian sat in a nearby chair. As they played, they talked, mostly at first about their days with the Volpolni Family Circus.

Ten years before, when they were both a part of that circus, they had met and fallen in love. Oren was in the high wire act then. Lillian rode beautiful white Arabian horses in her own act. They had both taken a great interest in an air show that had joined the circus for a while. By the time the circus closed in the summer of 1858, they had learned a lot about ballooning. That was when they decided to buy a balloon of their own and go on the road as a team.

The more Oren and Lillian talked about the past, the more they began to miss their balloon act in the *Benjamin Franklin*. For one thing, the Balloon Corps just wasn't as exciting as they had hoped. They knew they had given useful information to the army. But there had been long spaces of time when there was nothing to report. For another thing, they were used to free flights. Flying in a tied balloon was fine for a while, but not forever. Even now, after Oren had shown how important free flights might be, they were still not allowed.

Something else made Lillian and Oren think about returning to their air show. They hadn't been paid for a single Balloon Corps flight. Many of the aeronauts in the corps had complained to Professor Lowe about not being paid. Still nothing had been done. Most of the pilots had agreed to stay on. But the Barths had spent most of their savings while working for the army. They couldn't go on much longer without being paid.

Before long, Lillian and Oren decided to quit the Balloon Corps and go back on the road with their air show. As they waited for Oren's leg to get better, they planned how they would tell General Cooper and Professor Lowe. Then on May 29, as rain drenched the camp, General Cooper came to their tent. They invited him to sit, but he remained standing. Like everyone who had been outside, his clothes were dripping and his boots covered with mud.

"Problems, problems, and more problems," the general barked as he walked up and down in front of Lillian and Oren. "This rain is turning everything into a sea of mud. Men are dying left and right from the Chickahominy fever. And now Lincoln has sent McDowell's army to fight Stonewall Jackson. That means it might be weeks before Mac-Dowell and his men can join General McClellan to attack Richmond. And while we wait here, the Rebs might be planning to move against us."

"Us? You mean our army right here?" Oren asked.

"That's right," said General Cooper. "That Confederate General Joe Johnston isn't called 'Fighting Joe' for nothing. If he's half as smart as he is brave, he'll make a move as soon as the storm lets up. Could be he'll move against the Union's left. Or the right. But he might surprise us all and attack the rear— our camp right here."

Oren and Lillian looked at each other. It didn't seem the right time to tell General Cooper about wanting to leave. Not with all the other problems facing him.

General Cooper went on. "Knowing that Johnston might strike, we've got to be ready. I know the *Phoenix* was torn to bits, but you still have the *Benjamin Franklin*. And I know Oren shouldn't make a flight with his bad leg." The general stopped walking and looked straight at Lillian. "But you can," he said to her. "As soon as this rain stops, I'd like you to go up and see what the enemy is doing."

# 9

# **Fair Oaks**

*McClellan's biggest mistake was trying to hold both sides of the Chickahominy River. To do that, he cut his army in half. When the rain caused the river to climb its banks, the two sides were cut off from each other.*

*Confederate General Johnson attacked McClellan's left side as soon as the sun came out. The battle took place at a small rail station between Fair Oaks and Seven Pines.*

*All through the bloody battle, Professor Lowe flew his largest balloon,* Intrepid, *above the fighting. He telegraphed up-to-the-minute reports directly to General McClellan. And he gave orders to the artillery as well. His information did much to help Union forces. Years later Union General A. W. Greely would say that Professor Lowe's reports had been what saved the Union army from defeat at Fair Oaks.*

*Lowe's reports did indeed help a lot. But the Confederate's attack was not well carried out. Fighting Joe Johnston soon ran into trouble, and his soldiers were forced to pull back. The Union army was helped as much by Confederate mistakes as it was by Thaddeus Lowe.*

The rain had finally stopped, and the sky was clearing. It was early in the morning of the last day of May.

"Stand by your cables!" Lillian called the order to the ground crew. She stood in the gondola and waited as the grand *Benjamin Franklin* began to move.

Soon Lillian was high above the tops of the trees. She put her field glasses up to her eyes. As far as she could see there were no Confederate forces to the east or the south. Everything looked quiet.

Suddenly the *Benjamin Franklin* jerked to a stop, throwing Lillian to the floor of the gondola. As she tried to stand, the balloon started climbing again. Then shouts came from below.

Lillian grabbed the side of the swinging wicker basket and looked down toward the ground. One of the crew had got his leg wrapped in a line. Screaming, the man was being dragged slowly along.

As Lillian watched, the other soldiers in the ground crew let go of their lines and ran to help the trapped man. At the same time, someone who looked like Lieutenant Anderson ran forward and cut the line away from the screaming soldier's leg. Without thinking about it, they had set the *Benjamin Franklin* free. Lillian grabbed the side of the gondola even more tightly. The big balloon rose in the sky like a giant bird.

Higher and higher the balloon climbed, until Lillian thought it would never stop. She was above the clouds, and the air was cold, very cold, when the *Benjamin Franklin* finally stopped climbing.

Lillian let out a long breath and reached for a coat she had stored in the gondola. Then she picked up her field glasses. But there were no breaks in the clouds to see through. There was no way to tell how far she had gone or where she was. She could figure out from the sun, however, that the balloon was moving very fast toward the south.

Lillian would have to get below the clouds to find out where she was. Quickly she reached up and pulled a yellow rope that was connected to a valve in the top of the balloon. The valve opened, and a small amount of hydrogen escaped. Slowly the *Benjamin Franklin* began to sink.

Lillian let go of the rope when the balloon broke through the clouds. Now she could tell that she was about 2,000 feet high. She could see the James River far to the north. With a sinking feeling, she knew she was deep within enemy territory—and going deeper. The wind was pushing her farther and farther to the south.

Now that she knew where she was, Lillian decided to climb back above the clouds. She had to find a wind that would take her north. But in order to climb, she would have to get rid of some weight in the gondola. That meant dropping one of the 100-pound bags of sand that were tied to it.

Lillian put down her glasses and started to look for a knife to cut a bag free. But as she did, she caught sight of something strange on the ground. Looking through her field glasses again, she couldn't believe her eyes. There on the ground not five miles away was the *Phoenix*. It was the very same balloon that Oren had crashed behind Southern lines.

Now it was patched in many places and ready to fly again.

That balloon was named well, Lillian thought to herself as she floated closer to it. She remembered the old tales of the giant bird called the phoenix. It was said to have lived for 500 years. Every time it had died, it came back to life again. And now the Union's *Phoenix* had been born again too. Only this time it was under Rebel control.

As Lillian stared at the *Phoenix,* it pulled at its lines in the small clearing. A giant fire burned next to it. Lillian figured the Confederates were filling the balloon with hot smoke and air. She knew that the Southern forces had no way to make hydrogen.

Suddenly the *Phoenix* began to climb out of the clearing and into the air. It pulled hard at its lines and smoked like an angry dragon. As Lillian looked at it, it seemed to be coming straight at her.

Then she noticed something else. A man stood alone in the gondola below the balloon. A gun was in his hand. He was pointing it in her direction!

# 10

# End of the Beginning

*His name was John C. Calhoun Smith, and he was an officer in the Confederate army. He was named after a man who had been a great Southern leader for more than 50 years.*

*A few weeks before, Smith had been guarding supplies with the Confederate forces in Norfolk. He had hated that job and had longed for something more exciting. He had never dreamed, though, that he would be picked for the most dangerous and exciting job on the peninsula.*

*As his patched balloon climbed higher and closer to the Yankee aerostat, Smith smiled to himself. He had more than 50 guns with him in the gondola—all loaded and ready to fire. The guns had been given to him just before he took off. That was when his crew had first spotted the free-flying balloon coming their way. Now Smith was ready to use the guns. He planned to blow the Yankee balloonist out of the sky.*

*Bang!*

Lillian grabbed her knees and ducked inside the basket as a bullet cut through the air close to her head. The Rebel was a good shot. She would have to think fast if she wanted to stay alive.

*Bang!*

Another shot whistled by. Lillian peeked over the side to see how close she was to the Rebel balloon. It looked as if the *Phoenix* had reached the end of its line. And it looked as if Lillian was about to float directly over it. She would be a sitting duck for the Confederate soldier.

There wasn't time to cut loose enough sandbags to send the *Benjamin Franklin* climbing out of range of the Rebel's guns. Lillian could see he had many of them in his gondola. There was only one thing she could try. Quickly she reached for the anchor that was hanging from the side of her gondola. The anchor was usually used to bring about a faster landing. The heavy hook would dig into the earth and pull the balloon quickly after it. But now Lillian needed it for a different reason.

The *Benjamin Franklin* was passing right over the *Phoenix*. Lillian could see the Confederate soldier picking up another gun. Using all her strength, she pushed the anchor out of the gondola and sent it swinging toward the balloon below. It swung through the air like a pendulum on a giant clock. Then the sharp hook of the anchor cut into the *Phoenix* and held.

The winds pulled the *Benjamin Franklin* past the *Phoenix* as the anchor cut a large, long hole in the top of it. Hot smoke and air shot up out of the opening. Lillian held her breath and ducked into the gondola. Still the smoke burned in her eyes and made her cough. But she knew her plan had worked. She could hear the Southern soldier yelling as his balloon quickly fell to the ground.

But Lillian's trouble was still not over. Before long the soldiers on the ground would get over their surprise and start shooting at her again. She would have to climb fast. And she still had to find a good wind that would blow the *Benjamin Franklin* north and take her back to the camp.

As fast as she could, Lillian found her knife and cut two sandbags loose. She heard the heavy bags hit the ground as she started her fast climb away from the Confederates. Higher and higher she went, more than two miles above the ground.

Finally the *Benjamin Franklin* stopped climbing, and Lillian found a wind to take her north. With a long breath, she started to watch the beautiful trees through the breaks in the clouds. She was looking for a sight that would tell her she was close to camp.

Not long after, the James River came into view. Soon Lillian was back over the Union territory, and happy to be there. But now she had to figure out how to land without getting caught in all the trees. Suddenly Lillian had an idea.

She reached up to the rope that opened the valve to let the gas out. She pulled it, and slowly the balloon began to float toward the ground. Now she could see the Chickahominy River coming closer. As soon as she was over it, she let go of the valve rope and pulled hard on the red rope beside it.

A big hole was torn in the bottom of the balloon. The hydrogen escaped in a rush, sending the *Benjamin Franklin* toward the ground even faster. As the big balloon dropped, the wind pushed the torn bottom into the top. The *Benjamin Franklin* had turned into a giant parachute.

As she had done so often in the past, Lillian rode the parachute slowly down. But this time she landed in the Chickahominy River. And she and her balloon were pulled out by Union soldiers.

* * *

Lillian was back at the camp enjoying her first visit with Oren since her return. As they talked, General Cooper arrived at their tent. He sat down and nodded at them, then got right to the point.

"You'll both be going home soon," he said. "Professor Lowe heard about the free flights you both made. He has asked for you to leave the Balloon Corps. He says you were warned against taking free flights while you were working for him."

Oren started to turn purple. "But I did my flight to gather important information. And

Lillian's, well, that happened just because of an —"

Lillian put up her hand and broke in. "It's just as well, Oren," she said. "We had decided to leave anyway, remember?"

Oren caught his breath as he thought back to their decision. But that only made him think of one of the main reasons they had decided to quit.

"What about the money we're owed?" he asked General Cooper. "We haven't been paid anything for any of the flights we've made."

General Cooper nodded again. "You'll be paid before you leave," he said. But the general's mind was on other things. He was thinking about the days and weeks ahead. "Most likely there won't be time for much ballooning now, anyway," he said. "We'll be pulling back soon."

"Pulling back?" Oren quickly forgot his anger when he heard General Cooper's words. "But what about McClellan's attack on Richmond? What has happened?"

"While McClellan waited, Johnston attacked him at Fair Oaks this morning," the general said. "McClellan's men were hit hard. But nothing was really decided by the battle. Johnston was shot, and the Confederates had to pull back. Now the Rebels have asked Robert E. Lee to take command of their army."

"Robert E. Lee!" Oren said. He and Lillian looked at each other. They both knew that President Lincoln had asked Lee to lead the Union army when the war had first broken out. But Lee had turned the president down. He didn't want to fight against his home state of Virginia. Now the great general was going to command the Rebel forces instead.

General Cooper nodded once more. "Yes," he said. "Lee. He'll be leading the Confederates, and McClellan is in trouble. It looks like the war will go on much longer than we had hoped."

The tired-looking general smiled at Lillian and Oren. "But you've both done your part," he said to them. "I thank you for your help." Then the general turned and slowly left the tent. Outside, it began to rain again.